The Magic Rabbit

The Magic Rabbit

Annette LeBlanc Cate

CANDLEWICK PRESS

Second paperback edition 2013

The Library of Congress has cataloged the hardcover edition as follows:

Cate, Annette.
The magic rabbit / Annette LeBlanc Cate. — 1st ed.
p.   cm.
Summary: When Bunny becomes separated from Ray, a magician who is his business partner and friend,
he follows a crowd to a park where he has a lovely afternoon, and after the people leave and
darkness falls, the lonely and frightened Bunny finds a glittering trail of hope.
ISBN 978-0-7636-2672-3 (hardcover)
[1. Lost articles — Juvenile fiction. 2. Rabbits — Juvenile fiction. 3. Magicians — Juvenile fiction.
4. Lost and found possessions — Fiction. 5. Rabbits — Fiction. 6. Magicians — Fiction.]   I. Title.
PZ7.C268788 Mag 2007
[E] — dc22   2007022789

ISBN 978-0-7636-6685-9 (paperback)

15 16 17 APS 10 9 8 7 6 5 4

Printed in Humen, Dongguan, China

The text was hand-lettered by the author-illustrator.
The illustrations were done in ink and watercolor.

Candlewick Press
99 Dover Street
Somerville, Massachusetts 02144

visit us at www.candlewick.com

For Mom and Dad

THE MAGIC OF

EGYPT

Ray and Bunny lived together in a tiny apartment in the city. They were business partners. Ray was a magician, and Bunny was his loyal assistant.

THE Amazing Ray

STUFF FOR SHOW

They were also best friends. They did everything together.

Every Saturday, Ray and Bunny took their magic show downtown. But one Saturday, the sidewalk was a little more crowded than usual. And just as Ray said the magic word and Bunny was about to leap from the hat in a spray of glittering stars—

The scene became a terrible tangle of balls and stars, juggler and magician, hat and—
"Bunny? Bunny, where are you?" shouted Ray.
The hat was empty. Bunny was gone!

Meanwhile, the juggler's yipping pug was chasing Bunny down the sidewalk and right into the busy street!

Car horns blared. Bicycle bells rang.

People shouted at the bunny dodging in and out of traffic.

At last, Bunny made it across. He was safe now.

But where was Ray? All Bunny could see were legs and feet. Maybe if Bunny followed them, they would lead him back to Ray.

The feet led him to a beautiful, cool green park. It was a wonderful place for a little bunny, full of squirrels to frolic with and little bits of pretzel to nibble on. But no Ray.

As the sunlight faded away, so did everyone else. Bunny was all alone.

Bunny wandered along the dark street, thinking of Ray and wishing that they were sitting down to dinner together right now, at their own little table in the kitchen.

All around him, people were hurrying home to their own dinners. No one stopped or even seemed to notice the lost little bunny.

Bunny hopped along a little farther, then slipped down a dark alley to rest. He was tired and hungry and missed Ray terribly. A tear rolled down his nose. His nose twitched. Then... his nose twitched again. Bunny smelled something good to eat.

It was popcorn, his favorite!

Bunny got right to business. As he was nibbling, he noticed something shining among the kernels. Glittering stars! Lots of them!

Bunny followed the path
of stars out of the alley,

along the street...

up a hill...

down some stairs...

and through the subway station, all the way to...

his very own hat!

The last train of the night pulled away.
Only a magician and his bunny assistant were left on the platform.
But two old friends never mind walking home together.